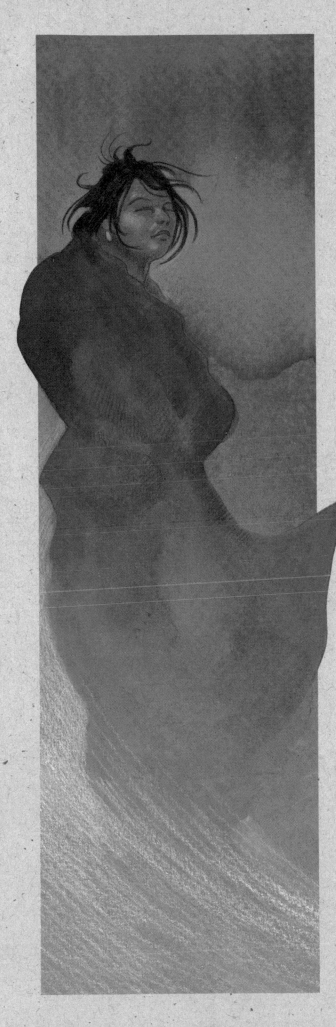

The Magic of Spider Woman

BY **LOIS DUNCAN**

ILLUSTRATED BY

SHONTO BEGAY

SCHOLASTIC INC.

New York Toronto London Auckland Sydney
Mexico City New Delhi Hong Kong

A Note About This Story

This story is about the legendary Navajo Spider Woman, a sacred being who taught the Navajo how to weave blankets so they could survive the cold during their first winter in North America.

Long before people wrote them down, legends passed orally from one generation to the next, so many different versions of Spider Woman's story exist today. Lois Duncan has drawn from several well-documented versions to create *The Magic of Spider Woman*. Though some of the circumstances may vary from ones with which you are familiar, Ms. Duncan has maintained the integrity of the legend as it was conceived to reinforce a most important concept of Navajo culture — the need for a well-balanced life.

ISBN 0-590-46156-7

Text copyright © 1996 by Lois Duncan.
Illustrations copyright © 1996 by Shonto Begay.
All rights reserved.
Published by Scholastic Inc.
SCHOLASTIC and associated logos are trademarks and/or registered trademarks of Scholastic Inc.

12 11 10 9 8   7 / 0

Printed in the U.S.A.   40

First Scholastic Trade paperback printing, October 2000

The display type was set in Pelican and the text type was set in Veljovic by WLCR New York Inc., New York, NY
Design by Marijka Kostiw

For Lily and Connor Bush
—L.D.

I Dedicate the Art
to all the guardians of
Spider Woman's spirit,
the weavers of the Dinéh Nation —
especially to my mother, Faye,
my Aunt Juanita,
and my late grandmother,
Bessie Smith
—S.B.

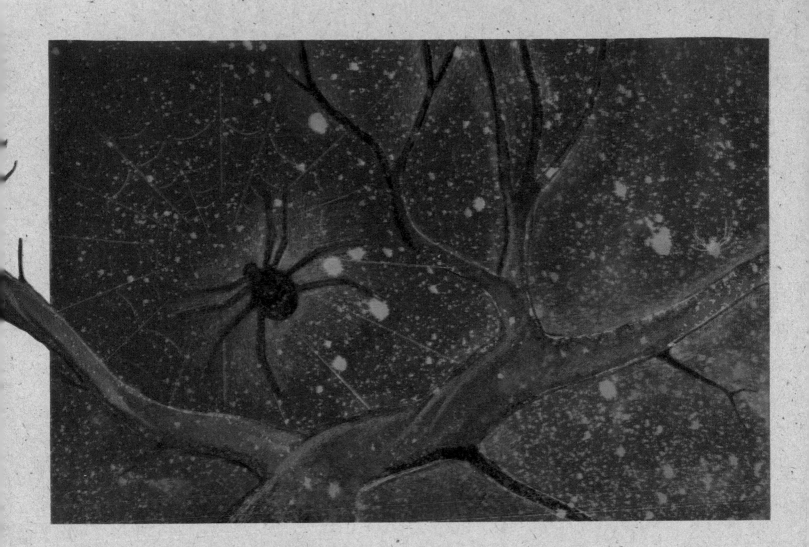

This is the story of Wandering Girl, who came to be known as Weaving Woman, and of the terrible thing that happened when she disobeyed Spider Woman.

And this is how the old ones told it.

Before the beginning of time there were only the animal beings and the insects who made their homes in the Third World.

One of the insect beings was Spider Woman, and she knew the secret of how to spin and to weave.

The Third World was flooded, but the animal beings and the insect beings escaped through a hollow reed, up into the Fourth World.

On the surface of the Fourth World, the beings discovered beauty they had never imagined when they lived in the chaos and the darkness of the Third World. Red clay mesas glowed in the morning sunlight, and valleys sparkled with wildflowers, and deep, green forests blanketed towering mountains.

"This world is too beautiful not to be shared," the animal beings told each other. The Spirit Being created the first people, who were called *Dinéh*, the Navajo.

Among the Navajo People there was one who was strong-willed and stubborn, and she was called Wandering Girl because she was a shepherd.

And there was one who loved Wandering Girl, and his name was Boy With a Dream.

Boy With a Dream watched with sadness as Wandering Girl led her sheep up into the mountains to graze in the high meadows, because his dream was to make Wandering Girl his wife.

The Spirit Being came to the Fourth World, which was on the earth's surface. It filled the earth, the sky, and the mountaintops until it was everywhere.

This Spirit Being spent the summer teaching all the People, except Wandering Girl, the things they needed to know to survive in the earth world. It taught them how to hunt game, how to grow crops, and how to build shelters called "hogans." But its most important teachings were the songs and chants called the Blessing Way that would keep the People healthy and in harmony with nature.

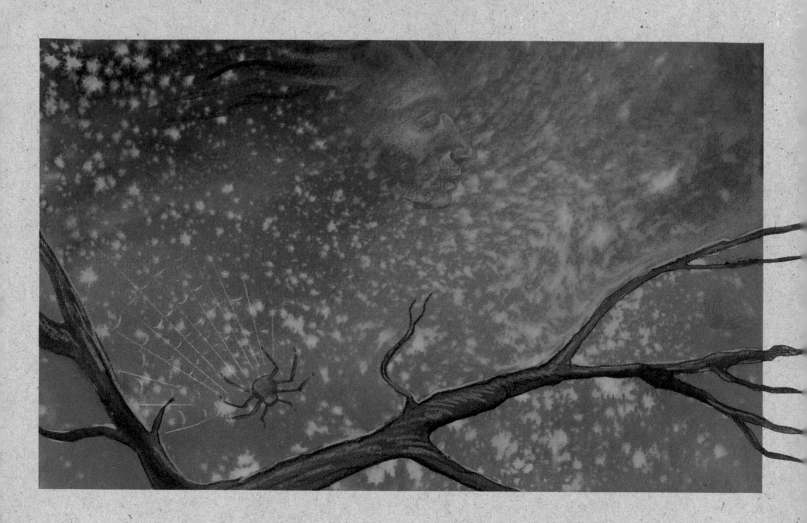

All through the warm, sweet summer Wandering Girl tended her flock in the high meadows, but when the tender grass grew brown and ice formed over the streams, she led her sheep back down the mountain to the Valley of the Spirit Being.

She expected to find her people waiting there to welcome her, but instead she was greeted by silence.

The People were in their hogans keeping warm by their fires.

Wandering Girl stood alone and shivered in the wind. She had no hogan to go to.

"Help me, Spirit Being!" she cried. "It is cold, and I am freezing!"

But it was Spider Woman who heard her and took pity on her.

"I will teach you how to make blankets from the wool of your sheep," she said. "Then you will be able to stay warm."

Spider Woman asked her husband to build a loom for Wandering Girl.

While he was doing this, Spider Woman showed Wandering Girl how to shear her sheep and to card and spin their wool. Then she taught her how to weave that wool into blankets.

"You are no longer a Wandering Girl," said Spider Woman. "Your place is now with the People. From this day on you are to be known as Weaving Woman, and you will weave warm blankets for the People, and this will bring you happiness.

"But there is one danger that you always must be aware of. The Navajo People must walk the Middle Way, which means that they must respect boundaries and try to keep their lives in balance. They should not do *too much* of anything. You must promise not to weave for too long, or a terrible thing will happen to you."

Weaving Woman gave that promise easily.

Then she frowned as she glanced about her at the snow-covered land.

"How can I weave outside in the winter?" she asked Spider Woman. "Ice will form on the spindles and freeze them to the wool."

Boy With a Dream overheard her and came out of his hogan, and his dream was singing in his heart.

"If you were my wife, my hogan would be yours," he told Weaving Woman. "You could set up the loom by the fire and the spindles would stay warm."

When Weaving Woman looked into his eyes and saw his love for her shining there, she put her life as Wandering Girl behind her.

"Then let us be married," she said, and opened her arms to him.

Then Boy With a Dream became Man Who Is Happy.

All through the winter, Weaving Woman kept her promise to Spider Woman. The blankets she wove were warm, but they were not very pretty, for they were made from the natural gray and brown wool of the sheep. She didn't mind laying aside her spindle after just a few hours at the loom, because the work she was doing was not exciting to her.

But when the snows melted and the air grew fresh and mild again, Weaving Woman asked her husband to move her loom outside so she could work in the sunshine. As the springtime world burst into glorious color all around her, she began to hear her loom sing, and she was no longer willing to weave with the drab shades of winter.

Instead, she made dyes out of roots and bark and berries, and she used these dyes to add rich colors to her weaving.

She wove the red of the mesas into her blankets. She wove in the white light of morning that shone from the East, and the golden glow of twilight that shone from the West. She wove in the blue of the happy skies of the South, and the black of the clouds from the North that brought rain to the desert.

She used those colors to turn her blankets into pictures.

Into one of her blankets she wove a picture of rainbows.

Into one of her blankets she wove a picture of mountains.

Into one of her blankets she wove a picture of birds and deer and buffalo, and of Man Who Is Happy hunting with his bow and arrow.

Then she had the most wonderful idea of all! She would weave a picture for the Spirit Being using every color in nature, and would create the most beautiful blanket in all of the world.

Weaving Woman grew so excited just thinking about the blanket that she couldn't get to sleep that night. She began to weave in the first light of morning, and when darkness fell she was still at work at her loom. She could not bear to stop. The next day she rose at dawn and wove until sundown. The following day she did the same. Her husband watched with worry in his heart.

"Remember the warning of Spider Woman!" he told her.

But Weaving Woman was as stubborn and strong-willed as ever, and she continued to weave even after the sun went down. She worked all night by the light of the blue-veined moon, and when morning came she was almost finished with the blanket.

"Only the border remains to be done," she told her husband.

Then, deep in his heart, Man Who Is Happy took for himself another name. That new name was Man Who Is Frightened.

When Man Who Is Frightened returned from the hunt that evening, he was not surprised to find that something terrible had happened. He found his wife lying on the ground at the base of her loom. Her eyes were closed, and her arms and legs were as stiff as her spindle. When her husband called out to her, she could not answer him.

Man Who Is Frightened gathered his wife into his arms and carried her into their hogan and laid her down on a pile of the blankets she had woven.

Then he called for a Hand Trembler who knew the secrets of sickness.

The Hand Trembler rubbed corn pollen on both Weaving Woman and himself. Then he took more pollen and rubbed it on the inner part of his own right arm, and he offered up a prayer.

"Tell us, Spirit Being, what is the matter with this woman!"

The Hand Trembler's hand began to shake, and magic filled the hogan.

Weaving Woman spoke, but her voice did not come from her mouth. It came from the blanket on the loom outside the doorway.

"I am here!" cried the voice. "I am trapped, and I cannot get out!"

When Man Who Is Frightened heard this, he became even more desperate and called for a Shaman to perform another healing ceremony. The Shaman ground up white and yellow corn and set the weaving tools in it to purify them. Then he swept up all the loose pieces of wool that were scattered outside the hogan and placed them also in the corn meal.

When this was done, the Shaman held a Blessing Way.

This was the prayer that he chanted:

"In the house made of dawn,
In the house made of twilight,
In the house made of dark cloud,
May Weaving Woman be restored to us!"

He offered up that prayer for a very long time, and no one could enter or leave the hogan while he did this.

After the Blessing was completed, the Shaman cocked his head as if he were listening to voices that no one else could hear. Then he turned to Man Who Is Frightened.

"Your wife has been struck with the weaving sickness," he told him. "She broke her promise to Spider Woman, and, just as she was warned, a terrible thing has happened. She has woven her spirit into her blanket."

Man Who Is Frightened stared at the blanket on the loom, and he saw the terrified spirit of his wife gazing back at him.

"Is there any way that she can be set free?" he asked frantically.

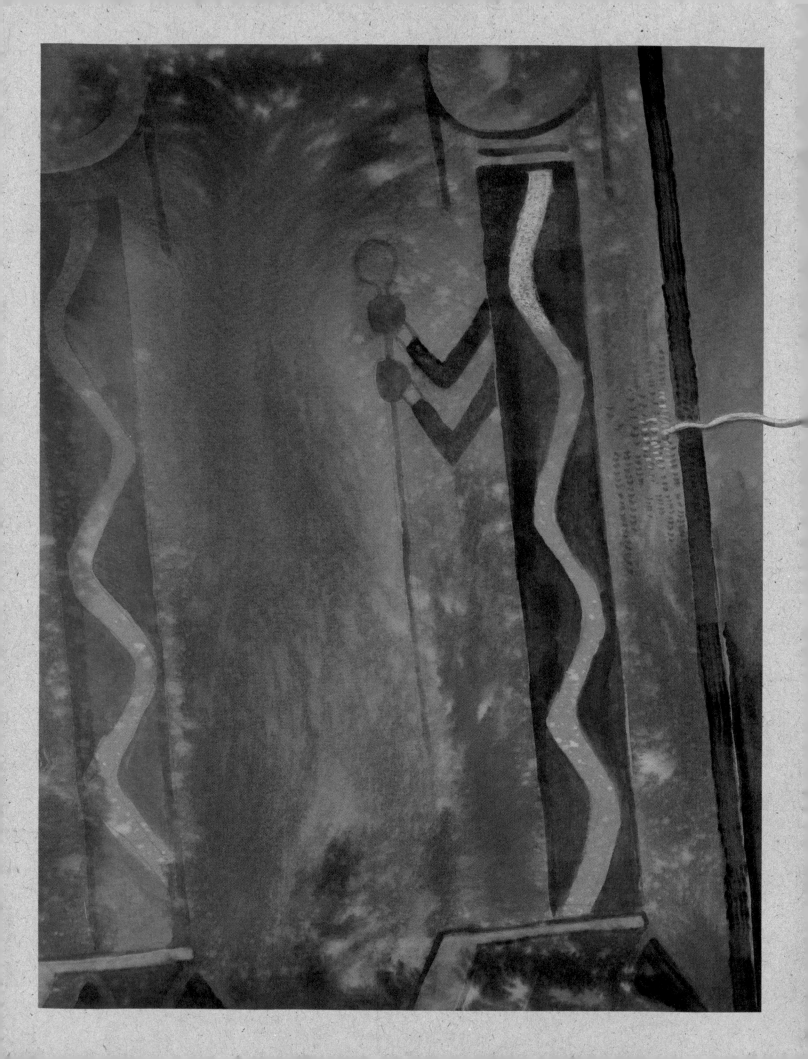

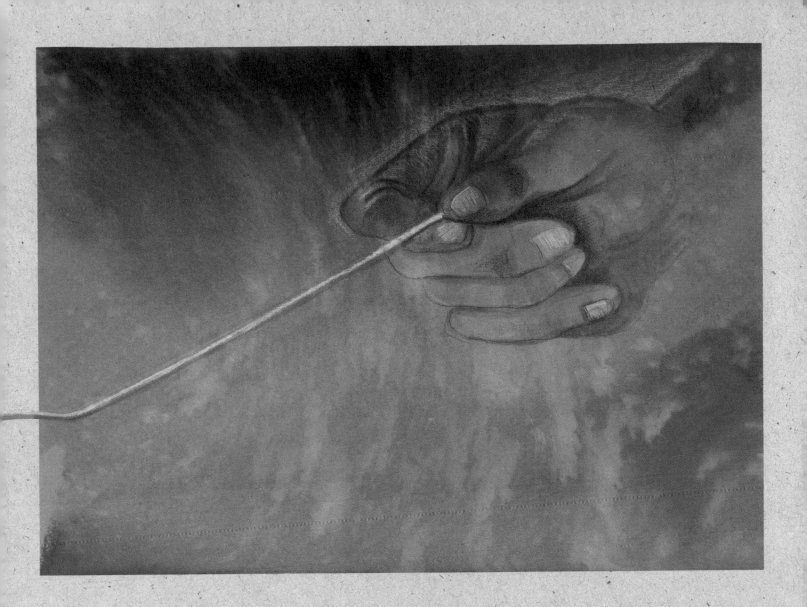

"Only if Spider Woman makes the blanket less perfect," said the Shaman. "And she cannot do that without the permission of the weaver."

Weaving Woman spoke again from the blanket.

"I beg you, Spider Woman, make the blanket less perfect!"

As Weaving Woman's plea filled the hogan, Spider Woman rose from the blanket and pulled loose a strand of the wool from the soft, gray background. She pulled the strand through the picture and opened a spirit pathway through the border of the blanket.

The spirit of Weaving Woman rushed down that pathway to freedom.

All because of the powerful magic of Spider Woman!

With her spirit now back in her body, Weaving Woman could see again, and her arms and legs could move again, and, when she spoke, her voice came out of her mouth.

"Oh, Spirit Being! I have learned my lesson!" she cried. "Never again will I weave for too long at a sitting, and never again will I doubt the wisdom of my creators."

Then Weaving Woman called together all the weavers of the land and had them sit on the ground at the base of her loom, while she taught them how to make spirit trails in their blankets by breaking the yarn and pulling a strand through the border.

"It is good to take pride in our work," she told them. "But we must not allow that pride to become master of our spirits."

So that is the story of Wandering Girl, who came to be known as Weaving Woman, and of the terrible thing that happened when she disobeyed Spider Woman.

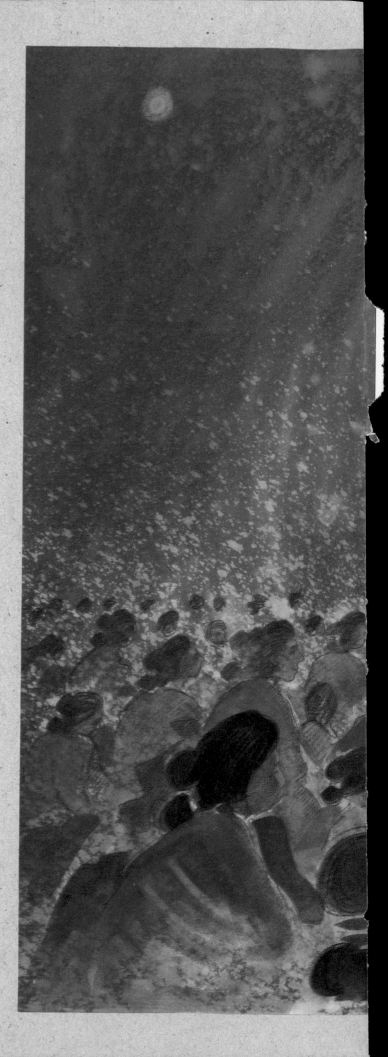

Since then, every Navajo blanket has been woven with a pathway, so the spirit of the weaver will not be imprisoned by its beauty.

The next time you see such a blanket, you should look at it carefully and remember the lesson of Spider Woman.

For this is how the old ones told it.